A Beginning-to-Read Book

It's Circus Time, Dear Dragon

WITHDRAWN

by Margaret Hillert

Illustrated by Jack Pullan

NORWOODHOUSE PRESS

DEAR CAREGIVER,

The books in this Beginning-to-Read collection may look somewhat familiar in that the original versions could have been a part of your own early reading experiences. These carefully written texts feature common sight words to provide your child multiple exposures to the words appearing most frequently in written text. These new versions have been updated and the engaging illustrations are highly appealing to a contemporary audience of young readers.

Begin by reading the story to your child, followed by letting him or her read familiar words and soon your child will be able to read the story independently. At each step of the way, be sure to praise your reader's efforts to build his or her confidence as an independent reader. Discuss the pictures and encourage your child to make connections between the story and his or her own life. At the end of the story, you will find reading activities and a word list that will help your child practice and strengthen beginning reading skills. These activities, along with the comprehension questions are aligned to current standards, so reading efforts at home will directly support the instructional goals in the classroom.

Above all, the most important part of the reading experience is to have fun and enjoy it!

Shannon Cannon

Shannon Cannon,
Literacy Consultant

Norwood House Press • www.norwoodhousepress.com
Beginning-to-Read™ is a registered trademark of Norwood House Press.
Illustration and cover design copyright ©2017 by Norwood House Press. All Rights Reserved.

Authorized adapted reprint from the U.S. English language edition, entitled It's Circus Time, Dear Dragon by Margaret Hillert. Copyright © 2017 Margaret Hillert. Reprinted with permission. All rights reserved. Pearson and It's Circus Time, Dear Dragon are trademarks, in the US and/or other countries, of Pearson Education, Inc. or its affiliates. This publication is protected by copyright, and prior permission to re-use in any way in any format is required by both Norwood House Press and Pearson Education. This book is authorized in the United States for use in schools and public libraries.

LIBRARY OF CONGRESS CATALOGING-IN-PUBLICATION DATA

Names: Hillert, Margaret, author. I Pullan, Jack, illustrator.
Title: It's circus time, Dear Dragon / by Margaret Hillert ; illustrated by Jack Pullan.
Other titles: It is circus time, Dear Dragon
Description: Chicago, IL : Norwood House Press, [2016] I Series: A
  beginning-to-read book I Summary: "A boy and his dragon go to the circus
  where Dear Dragon performs circus tricks and puts on a show of his own.
  Completely re-illustrated from original edition. Includes reading
  activities and a word list"-- Provided by publisher.
Identifiers: LCCN 2015046740 (print) I LCCN 2016014726 (ebook) I ISBN
  9781599537726 (library edition : alk. paper) I ISBN 9781603578981 (eBook)
Subjects: I CYAC: Dragons--Fiction. I Circus--Fiction.
Classification: LCC PZ7.H558 Is 2016 (print) I LCC PZ7.H558 (ebook) I DDC
  [E]--dc23
LC record available at http://lccn.loc.gov/2015046740

288N—072016
Manufactured in the United States of America in North Mankato, Minnesota.

I see it.
I see it.
Run, run, run!
This is something we will like.

Look at that.
Look up, up, up.
That is pretty.

And here come the funny ones.
Look here.
Look, look, look.

Now look here.
Oh, my.
Oh, my.
What is this?

I see something big.
Big, big, big.
But I do not see dragon.
Where is dragon?

9

Oh, no!
What do I see now?
Come here.
Come here.
You can not do that.

Come with me.
How funny you are!
But you can not do that.

Now we have to go in here.
This is where it is.
Come on in here.

This is a good spot for us.
Look what we can see.
What a good spot this is.

Oh, no!
How did you get way up there?
That is not a good spot for you.
Come down. Come down.
I did not come here
to see you do something.
I want you here with me.

Now what is this?
What do I see?
What are you on?

You are good at that.
Yes, you are pretty good.
But I want you here.
Come here now.

Not there. Not there.
Do not do that.
I want you to come here to me.

Oh, oh.
Look at you.
Look what you have on.
You are so funny.

And now look at you.
See what you can do.
You can help
this one jump.
My, what a jump!

But we have to go now.
Mother and Father want us.
Come on.
We have to go.

Here is something pretty.
I want a red one.
You can have one, too.

Mother!
Father!
Look at us.
See what we have.

Yes, yes.
We see what you have.
What fun for you.

Here you are with me.
And here I am with you.

Oh, what a happy day,
Dear Dragon.

READING REINFORCEMENT

The following activities support the findings of the National Reading Panel that determined the most effective components for reading instruction are: Phonemic Awareness, Phonics, Vocabulary, Fluency, and Text Comprehension.

Phonemic Awareness: The /t/ sound

Oddity Task: Say the /t/ sound for your child. Ask your child to say the word that doesn't have the /t/ sound in the following word groups:

tap, cap, pat	pod, pot, top	sip, pit, sit	pit, pat, pan
seam, seat, set	time, lime, tike	blue, to, stew	net, not, nod

Phonics: The letter Tt

1. Demonstrate how to form the letters **T** and **t** for your child.
2. Have your child practice writing **T** and **t** at least three times each.
3. Ask your child to point to the words in the book that have the letter **t** in them.
4. Write down the following words and ask your child to circle the letter **t** in each word:

not	too	not	little	to	that
get	want	this	what	tail	turtle

Vocabulary: Verbs

1. Explain to your child that words that describe actions are called verbs.
2. Write the following verbs from the story on separate pieces of paper:

run	look	see	come
go	get	do	help

3. Read each word to your child and ask your child to repeat it.
4. Mix the words up. Point to a word and ask your child to read it. Provide clues if your child needs them. Ask your child to describe him or herself using the verbs.

5. Read the following sentences to your child. Ask your child to provide an appropriate verb to complete the sentence.
   - There is the circus tent, hurry let's (run) to get there fast.
   - Can you (see) the big tent?
   - (Look) over there! It's a circus parade.
   - Would you like to (get) a balloon?
   - There are so many things to (see/do) at the circus.
   - It's time for us to (go) home.

Fluency: Choral Reading

1. Reread the story with your child at least two more times while your child tracks the print by running a finger under the words as they are read. Ask your child to read the words he or she knows with you.

2. Reread the story aloud together. Be careful to read at a rate that your child can keep up with.

3. Repeat choral reading and allow your child to be the lead reader and ask him or her to change from a whisper to a loud voice while you follow along and change your voice.

Text Comprehension: Discussion Time

1. Ask your child to retell the sequence of events in the story.

2. To check comprehension, ask your child the following questions:
   - What were all the things Dear Dragon did that the boy did not want him to?
   - What did Dear Dragon do to help in the circus?
   - What was your favorite part of the story? Why?
   - If you could be in a circus, what would you like to do? Why?

WORD LIST

***It's Circus Time, Dear Dragon* uses the 67 words listed below.**
This list can be used to practice reading the words that appear in the text. You may wish to write the words on index cards and use them to help your child build automatic word recognition. Regular practice with these words will enhance your child's fluency in reading connected text.

a	Father	jump	red	want
am	for		run	way
and	fun	like		we
are	funny	look	see	what
at			so	where
	get	me	something	will
big	go	Mother	spot	with
but	good	my		
			that	yes
can	happy	no	the	you
come	have	not	there	
	help	now	this	
day	here		to	
dear	how	oh	too	
did		on		
do	I	one (s)	up	
down	in		us	
dragon	is	pretty		
	it			

ABOUT THE AUTHOR Margaret Hillert has helped millions of children all over the world learn to read independently. She was a first grade teacher for 34 years and during that time started writing books that her students could both gain confidence in reading and enjoy. She wrote well over 100 books for children just learning to read. As a child, she enjoyed writing poetry and continued her poetic writings as an adult for both children and adults.

Photograph by Glenna Washburn

ABOUT THE ILLUSTRATOR A talented and creative illustrator, Jack Pullan, is a graduate of William Jewell College. He has also studied informally at Oxford University and the Kansas City Art Institute. He was mentored by the renowned watercolor artists, Jim Hamil and Bill Amend. Jack's work has graced the pages of many enjoyable children's books, various educational materials, cartoon strips, as well as many greeting cards. Jack currently resides in Kansas.